CUPHEAD © and ™ 2022 StudioMDHR Entertainment Inc.

THE CUPHEAD SHOW! ™ Based on the video game from StudioMDHR.

Netflix™: Netflix, Inc. Used with permission.

Published in the United States by Random House Children's Books, a division of Penguin Random House LLC, 1745 Broadway, New York, NY 10019, and in Canada by Penguin Random House Canada Limited, Toronto. Random House and the colophon are registered trademarks of Penguin Random House LLC.

RHCBOOKS.COM

Library of Congress Cataloging-in-Publication Data is available upon request.

ISBN 978-0-593-43204-4 (trade) — ISBN 978-0-593-43205-1 (ebook)

Printed in the United States of America

10 9 8 7 6 5 4 3 2 1

THE CUPHEAD SHOW!

HERE COMES TROUBLE!

FEATURING

"DANGEROUS MUGMAN"

AND

"GHOSTS AIN'T REAL"

RANDOM HOUSE NEW YORK

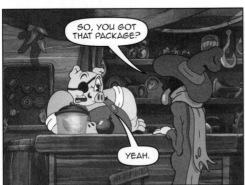

SO, YOU GOT THAT PACKAGE?

YEAH.

ONE BOX OF GRENADES.

TWO SACKS OF GUNPOWDER.

A SPOOL OF PIANO WIRE.

AND ONE TUBE OF TOOTHPASTE. SPEARMINT.

NOBODY PROCURES BLACK-MARKET GOODS LIKE YOU DO, PORKRIND.

SHH! DON'T USE MY REAL NAME!

I LIKE TO KEEP A LOW PROFILE.

DING!

HI, PORKRIND!

PING!

CLANK!

DING! BA-BING!

DANGER! DANGER!

7

HANDS OFF!

WHAT ABOUT THIS?

CLASSIFIED!

=GROAN=

WHOA! PORKRIND! A SHOE!

ONE TIME I FOUND A SHOE ON THE ROAD AND PUT IT ON MY FOOT.

THE SHOE I FOUND WAS TOO SMALL, BUT I LOVED IT ANYWAY BECAUSE I LOST MY SHOE EARLIER.

AND IT POPPED RIGHT ON!

THEN I REALIZED THAT THE SHOE I FOUND IN THE ROAD *WAS* MY SHOE.

GRRRR!

AND IT WASN'T TOO SMALL AFTER ALL-- JUST A FAMILY OF MICE LIVING INSIDE. I NAMED THEM.

DING! PING! CLANK! BA-BING!

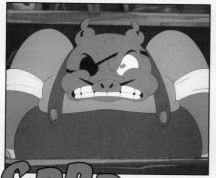

SMASH

WHUMP

HAHAHAHA!

PORKRIND!
PORKRIND!

14

I CAN SENSE WITHIN YOU THE BRAVERY REQUIRED TO COMPLETE THIS MISSION.

YOU, NOT SO MUCH.

WELL, I TAKE OFFENSE. I COULD BE DANGEROUS TOO. *HMPH!*

YEAH. DON'T WAIT UP FOR US.

I'M NOT DANGEROUS. HOW COULD I SAY THAT? WE GOTTA BACK OUT! I'M NOT UP FOR THIS!

16

CONFIDENCE AND BRAVERY?

YEAH! CUPHEAD, I'M FEELING A LITTLE DANGEROUS.

THAT'S THE SPIRIT!

NEXT STOP, MT. ERUPTUS!

FWISH FWISH FWISH FWISH

COME ON, CUPHEAD! WE GOTTA PROVE PORKRIND WRONG!

MAYBE WE'VE HAD ENOUGH DANGER FOR ONE DAY?

WE DON'T EVEN KNOW WHAT THIS DELICATE PACKAGE IS!

OH, YES, WE DO!

EGGS ARE DELICATE PACKAGES.

R·R·RUMBLE

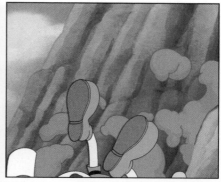

IF WE DON'T TURN BACK, WE'RE GONNA DIE!

TRUST THE GOGGLES. THEY HAVEN'T FAILED US YET.

YOU LOST THE GOGGLES! YOU HAVEN'T BEEN WEARING THEM FOR HOURS!

NO...NO GOGGLES?

NO GOGGLES?!

THIS IS BAD. THIS IS BAD!

AAAAAAAAAHHHHHHHHHHHH

WHUMP

I'M SORRY, MUGSY. I SHOULDA TOLD YOU THE GOGGLES CAME OFF. NOW WE'RE GONNA DIE!

WAIT. IF I WASN'T WEARING THE GOGGLES, THAT MEANS I DID ALL THAT DANGEROUS STUFF WITHOUT THEM!

DON'T YOU SEE, CUPHEAD? THE GOGGLES WERE INSIDE ME THIS WHOLE TIME!

GROSS.

BUT I SEE YOUR POINT.

WATCH THIS.

SMASH

SLAM!

HERE'S YOUR DELICATE PACKAGE, MY GOOD SIR.

WHERE HAVE YOU GUYS BEEN? YOU WERE GONE FOR THREE DAYS.

WELL, WHAT DO YOU EXPECT? YOU SENT US TO THE TOP OF MT. ERUPTUS.

NOT *THE* MT. ERUPTUS.

Mt. ERUPTUS CLEANERS

NO STAINS TOO STUBBORN!

MT. ERUPTUS CLEANERS!

MT. ERUPTUS CLEANERS? OH!

OH, WELL!

I GUESS THERE'S ONLY ONE THING LEFT TO DO, THEN.

TIME TO BREAK MY HIGH SCORE!

UH, CUPHEAD?

WHAT IS IT, MUGSY?

I'M FEELING A LITTLE... DANGEROUS.

NICKEL ME.

OH, NO, YOU DON'T!

HERE! TAKE IT! AND GET OUT!

THANK YOU, PORKRIND!

NOW PLAYING

HIDEOUS ZOMBIES!

HA-HA-HA
HA-HA!

ZOMBIES ARE NOT AS
SCARY AS I THOUGHT
THEY'D BE.

I'M PROUD OF YA,
MUGSY. YOU ONLY
NEEDED TO CHANGE
YOUR PANTS THREE
TIMES.

A NEW
RECORD.

OH! IT'S LATE. TO MAKE IT HOME BEFORE DARK, WE BETTER TAKE A SHORTCUT THROUGH THE CREEPY CEMETERY.

NOTHING SCARY ABOUT THAT. NOT TO A RECORD-BREAKER LIKE ME.

ATTABOY, MUGSY.

HMM.

SURE IS A LOT OF TOMBSTONES.

UH-HUH.

REALLY STARTING TO GET DARK NOW.

SOME MIGHT FIND THAT UNSETTLING, BUT NOT ME.

GOOD THING WE'RE SO BRAVE.

I CAN'T THINK OF A TIME I'VE BEEN LESS SCARED.

NOTHING SCARY ABOUT A GRAVEYARD.

IT'S JUST A YARD.

A YARD IS FOR PLAYING.

WE HAVE A YARD AT HOME.

WE SHOULD VACATION HERE.

WE SHOULD LIVE HERE!

I NEVER WANNA LEAVE!

CRAAACK

AAAAAHHH!

AAAAAHHH!

WELL, I KNOW WHAT WE'RE DOING TONIGHT.

THINGS JUST GOT A LOT MORE INTERESTING.

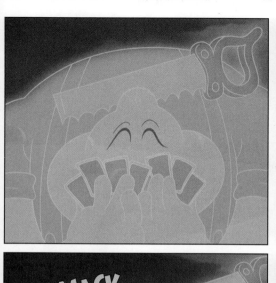

GO FISH!

SMACK

SLAM

HMM, STUCK PRETTY GOOD.

WHAT ARE WE GONNA DO?!

FIRST, WE'RE GONNA CALM DOWN.

BUT WHAT ABOUT GH-GH-GHOSTS?

AH, BANANA OIL! GHOSTS AIN'T REAL!

YOU HEAR THAT? WE AIN'T REAL. HEH-HEH.

I DON'T LIKE THIS, CUPHEAD. I'M ALLERGIC TO DEAD PEOPLE.

FOR THE LAST TIME, MUGSY. GHOSTS AIN'T REAL!

NOW YOU CLEAR A SPOT, AND I'M GONNA GET SOME FIREWOOD.

WE'RE SEPARATING?

WELL, DO YOU WANNA COME WITH ME INTO THE DEEP, DARK WOODS?

IS THERE A THIRD, LESS TERRIFYING OPTION?

LOOK, DON'T WORRY. IT'LL BE JUST LIKE THE MOVIES. YOU THINK YOU'RE GONNA BE SCARED, BUT THEN IT WON'T BE SO BAD.

'CAUSE WHY?

'CAUSE I'M A BIG, STRONG MAN?

WELL, SURE. BUT ALSO BECAUSE GHOSTS AIN'T REAL.

THEY BETTER NOT BE. I'M ALL OUTTA SPARE PANTS.

TYPICAL MUGMAN. ALWAYS GETTING HIMSELF WORKED UP OVER NOTHING.

SNAP

WHAT WAS THAT?

THWACK

OWW.

HUH?

HELLO.

AAAAHHH!

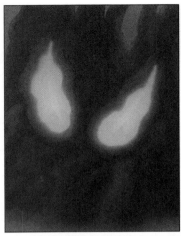

FIREFLIES. CUPHEAD WAS RIGHT. GHOSTS AIN'T REAL.

YOU KNOW, IT'S ACTUALLY KINDA PEACEFUL OUT HERE. JUST THE SOUNDS OF THE WIND, THE OWL, THE--

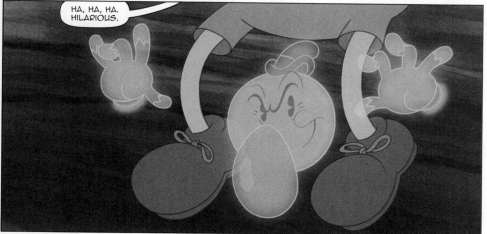

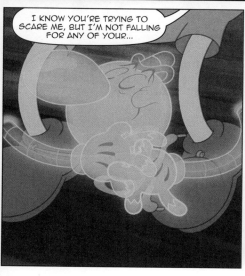

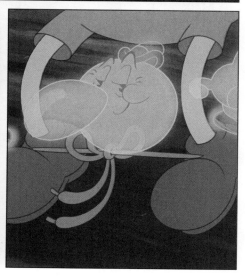

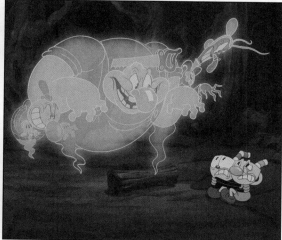

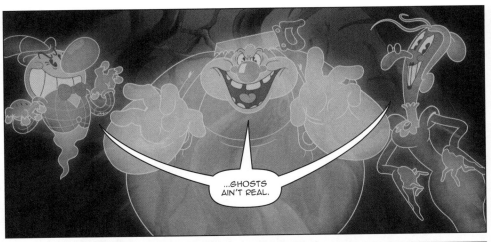

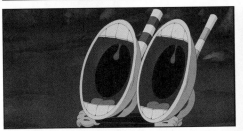

SMOOCH

SMASH

CRASH

SLAM

OVER HERE. OVER HERE.

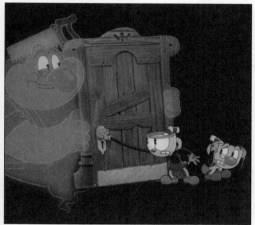

BLAAARG

SLAM

AAAAHHH!

WHUMP

NOW DO YOU BELIEVE IN--

÷GASP÷

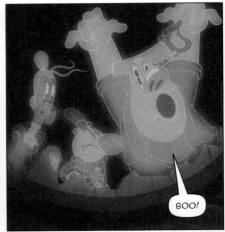

BOO!

KNOCK IT OFF. WE GOT A REAL PROBLEM HERE.

SMACK

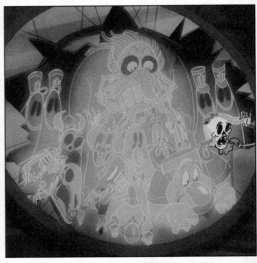

ONE MINUTE, WE'RE ALL HAVING FUN. THE NEXT MINUTE, TWO CUPS ARE DEAD.

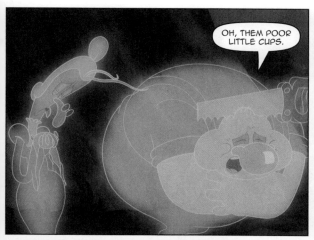

SLAM

PANT
PANT

WE MADE IT.

SAFE
AT LAST.

PHEW!

NETFLIX

THE CUPHEAD SHOW!

EXECUTIVE PRODUCER – DAVE WASSON

EXECUTIVE PRODUCER – CJ KETTLER

EXECUTIVE PRODUCER – CHAD MOLDENHAUER

EXECUTIVE PRODUCER – JARED MOLDENHAUER

CO-EXECUTIVE PRODUCER – COSMO SEGURSON

BASED ON THE VIDEO GAME BY STUDIO MDHR

DEVELOPED BY DAVE WASSON

SUPERVISING DIRECTOR – CLAY MORROW

SUPERVISING DIRECTOR – ADAM PALOIAN

WRITTEN BY – DEEKI DEKE

ART DIRECTOR – ANDREA FERNANDEZ

BOOK DESIGN – NEIL ERICKSON